Brave Hong Kil-dong

용감한 홍길동

The Man Who Bought
the Shade of a Tree

나무그늘을 산 총각

HOLLYM

Brave Hong Kil-dong

A long time ago in the Land of Morning Calm lived a brave young man named Hong Kil-dong.

The people of this era were divided into two groups —aristocrats and commoners. The aristocrats had government jobs and wealth, but the commoners had to work for the aristocrats and struggle to survive.

Kil-dong was the second son of a high-ranking aristocrat called Minister Hong, but because his mother was his father's servant, he could not openly call his father by the title "Father."

용감한 홍길동

옛날, 조선시대에 홍길동이라는 씩씩한 소년이 있었습니다.

홍길동이 살던 그 때는 사람들이 양반과 상민으로 나뉘어 있었습니다.

양반은 벼슬을 하고 많은 재산을 가졌지만, 상민은 양반 밑에서 일을 해주며 가난하게 살았습니다.

길동은 홍 판서라는 양반의 둘째 아들로 태어났으나, 어머니가 홍 판서의 종이었기 때문에 아버지를 아버지라고 부르지 못했습니다.

It was quite clear to everyone from the start that Kil-dong was exceptionally smart. Not surprisingly, all the other people in the household were jealous and hated him.

Kil-dong studied very hard. But as he grew older, he came to realize that a government position was impossible for a person like him who was not an aristocrat.

"Since I cannot get a proper and respectable job in the government," he thought, "I suppose I should leave this house and look for another line of work." And so he packed up his belongings and secretly left his father's house.

Kil-dong wandered aimlessly all over the country until one day he collapsed out of exhaustion somewhere deep in the mountains.

그러나 길동은 어려서부터 남달리 영리했습니다.

집안 사람들은 그런 길동을 몹시 미워하고 시기했습니다.

길동은 열심히 공부를 했습니다.

그러나 나이가 들면서 양반이 아닌 사람은 아무리 똑똑해도 벼슬을 할 수 없다는 것을 알게 되었습니다.

"벼슬을 하여 옳은 일을 할 수 없으니 차라리 집을 나가 다른 일을 찾아보자."

이렇게 마음먹은 길동은 짐을 꾸려서 몰래 집을 나왔습니다.

집을 나와 여기저기를 헤매던 길동은 어느 산 속에서 지쳐 쓰러졌습니다.

He was so tired he fell immediately asleep and slept until he was awakened by a voice calling to him.

He opened his eyes to see a mysterious old man with a long flowing white beard standing in front of him.

"Kil-dong," said the old man, "starting today, you are going to study the classics and learn military arts under me."

From that moment on, Kil-dong studied the classics and practiced military arts diligently. One year went by. And then a second. And then a third.

And then, after many months had gone by, the old man called Kil-dong to his side. "You are now an expert in both military arts and the classics," said the old man. "I can teach you no more. It's time for you to go out into the world and be a leader. You must do good deeds and serve others."

얼마 동안 쓰러져서 잠을 자던 길동은 누군가가 부르는 소리에 깨어났습니다.

길동의 앞에는 하얗고 긴 수염을 늘어뜨린 노인이 서 있었습니다.

"길동아, 너는 오늘부터 내 밑에서 글공부를 하면서 무술을 익히거라."
노인은 이렇게 말했습니다.

그날부터 길동은 열심히 공부를 하며 무술을 닦았습니다.

한 해, 두 해, 세 해……

오랜 세월이 지난 어느 날, 노인은 길동을 불렀습니다.

"이제 너의 무술과 학문이 훌륭해졌으니, 세상에 나가 좋은 일에 앞장서도록 하여라."

After bidding farewell to his master, Kil-dong came down from the mountain. He stopped at a small village where there was a celebration going on. All the people gathered there were very loud and growing louder.

Kil-dong moved in closer to find a gang of rowdy men testing their strength against an enormous rock. A tough-looking man walked up to him, grabbed him by the throat, and demanded, "Who are you and what are you doing here?"

"I heard all this loud noise," Kil-dong explained.

"Oh yeah? Then why don't you take your turn and try your luck at lifting that rock over there?"

산을 내려온 길동은 어느 조그만 마을에 이르렀습니다.

그 마을은 무슨 잔치가 벌어졌는지 사람들이 모여 웅성거리고 있었습니다.

길동이 가까이 가 보니 우락부락한 사나이들이 커다란 바윗덩어리를 놓고 힘을 겨루고 있었습니다.

그 때 험상스러운 사나이가 다가와 길동의 멱살을 잡고 물었습니다.

"너는 누군데 이곳에 왔느냐?"

"시끄러운 소리가 나길래 들었소."

"그래? 그럼 너도 저 바위를 한번 들어 볼 테냐?"

Without the slightest show of effort, Kil-dong calmly lifted the huge rock and threw it far off into the distance.

The gang of men couldn't believe their eyes. Their mouths fell open in astonishment.

"Hey, big brother...mister...sir," they called out. "Please join us and become our leader." The gang of men threw themselves on the ground and bowed deeply to Kil-dong.

"I don't want to be the leader of a gang of thieves," said Kil-dong. "But any of you who wants to do right can follow me."

On that day, Kil-dong took charge of a large and loyal band of men.

길동은 커다란 바위를 번쩍 들어 멀리 내던졌습니다.

우락부락한 사나이들은 놀라서 입을 딱 벌렸습니다.

"아이쿠 형님, 저희들의 두목이 되어 주십시오."

사나이들은 모두 넙죽 엎드려 길동에게 절을 했습니다.

"나는 도둑의 두목이 되고 싶지 않소. 모두들 옳은 일을 하려거든 나를 따르시오."

그 날부터 홍길동은 많은 부하를 거느리게 되었습니다.

Kil-dong decided one day to travel to a Buddhist temple which was filled with wicked monks. Dressed and acting like the son of a very important man, he easily fooled the monks.

At dinner time, he put pebbles in his mouth as he was eating. With a lot of motion, he chewed loudly for all to hear.

"You devils!" he screamed. "You deliberately put stones in my food to have your fun with me. Didn't you?" He turned his head and shouted, "Tie up all these monks."

At this command, his men rushed inside. They caught and tied the monks. Then they carried all of the rice and treasures outside.

"How can a temple have so many riches?" Kil-dong scolded the monks. "I don't think you got them honestly."

어느 날, 길동은 못된 중들이 모여 사는 절을 찾아갔습니다.

홍길동은 높은 사람의 아들처럼 꾸미고 중들을 속였습니다.

저녁 때가 되어 밥을 먹던 홍길동은 일부러 돌을 '와드득' 씹었습니다.

"이놈들이 나를 놀리려고 일부러 돌을 넣었구나. 어서 이 중들을 묶어라."

그러자 홍길동의 부하들이 우르르 달려들어 중들을 묶고, 절에 있던 쌀과 재물을 모두 밖으로 꺼내 놓았습니다.

"절에 무슨 재물이 이렇게 많으냐? 못된 짓으로 모은 것이 틀림없으렸다!"

홍길동은 중들을 꾸짖었습니다.

Kil-dong   evenly distributed the rice and treasures he had taken from the temple among the poor people.

"From now on, we will rob from the rich and give to the poor," he told his men. "We're going to punish bad people and help poor people."

At this time, there were many rumors about a government official in Hamgyong Province who cheated the people. Kil-dong led his band of men there. They found the people in starving, doing all they could to stay alive.

홍길동은 절에서 빼앗은 쌀과 재물을 가난한 사람들에게 나눠 주었습니다.

그러고나서 부하들에게 말했습니다. "이제부터 우리를 '활빈당'이라고 부르겠소. 나쁜 무리들을 혼내 주고 가난한 백성들을 도와 줍시다."

그 무렵에 함경도에 사는 벼슬아치가 백성을 괴롭힌다는 소문이 떠돌았습니다.

홍길동은 활빈당을 이끌고 함경도로 떠났습니다.

함경도 땅에 이르니, 그 곳 사람들은 모두 굶주려서 겨우겨우 목숨을 이어가고 있었습니다.

Kil-dong went straight to the house of the province's inspector and set fire to it.

While they ran around in confusion trying to put out the fire, Kil-dong and his men ran into the inspector's warehouse to take all the grain and treasures that were neatly stacked in piles.

Kil-dong's outlaw band became a sensation throughout the entire country.

"You mean to say there's a man named Hong Kil-dong who gives grain to poor people?"

"They say he goes around making trouble for government officials." "I didn't know such a wonderful fellow could exist in this world."

Whenever people gathered together, they would praise Hong Kil-dong.

홍길동은 함경 감사의 집에 불을 지르게 했습니다.

사람들이 불을 끄려고 어수선한 틈을 타서 홍길동과 부하들은 창고에 쌓인 곡식과 재물을 모두 꺼내가지고 달아났습니다.

온 나라 안이 활빈당때문에 떠들썩해졌습니다.

"홍길동이라는 사람이 가난한 사람들에게 곡식을 나눠 준다면서?"

"나쁜 벼슬아치들을 혼내주고 다닌대요."

"세상에, 그렇게 훌륭한 사람이 어디 있담!"

백성들은 입을 모아 홍길동을 칭찬했습니다.

At the very mention of his name, rich people and government officials would begin to tremble in fear.

Eventually, even the king heard the stories about Hong Kil-dong. He summoned his best general, a man famous for his cleverness, and ordered him to capture the outlaw.

The general went out in search of Hong Kil-dong. While crossing a mountain pass, he met a youg man.

"General, aren't you looking for Hong Kil-dong?" the young man asked. "If you are, follow me."

The general thought this odd, but shrugged and followed the man to the edge of a cliff.

The young man sat down, turned his back to the general, and said, "Now go ahead and kick me as hard as you can."

부자들과 벼슬아치들은 홍길동의 이름만 들어도 벌벌 떨었습니다.

임금님도 홍길동의 소문을 듣고 날쌘 장군을 시켜 잡아오게 했습니다.

홍길동을 잡으러 나선 장군은 어느 고갯마루에서 한 소년을 만났습니다.

"장군님, 홍길동을 잡으러가는 길이지요? 그럼 저를 따라오세요."

이상하게 여긴 장군은 소년의 뒤를 따라 낭떠러지 끝으로 갔습니다.

소년은 낭떠러지 끝에 등을 돌리고 앉아 장군에게 말했습니다.

"자, 이제 내 등을 힘껏 차 보세요."

In a sudden surge of anger, the general kicked the young man's back with all of his might.

But the young man's body did not even move. "How could a Korean general possibly be so weak?" The young man laughed. "I am the Hong Kil-dong you're looking for."

Kil-dong tied up the general and left him dangling from a pine tree. The general returned home in disgrace. When the king heard how his best general had been tricked and treated, he was furious.

Notices offering a big reward for the capture of Hong Kil-dong were posted all over the country. Nevertheless, Hong Kil-dong would show up in the east, and then in the west, making life miserable for bad people.

장군은 화가 치밀어서 소년의 등을 냅다 찼습니다.

그러나 소년은 꼼짝도 하지 않았습니다.

"하하하하……. 한 나라의 장군이 이렇게 약해서야 되겠소? 내가 바로 홍길동이요."

홍길동은 장군을 꽁꽁 묶어 소나무에 매달았습니다.

장군이 홍길동에게 혼이 나고 돌아오자, 임금님은 몹시 화가 났습니다.

온 나라 안에 홍길동을 잡으면 큰 상을 준다는 방이 나붙었습니다.

그러나 홍길동은 동에 나타났다, 서에 나타났다 하면서 여전히 나쁜 사람들을 혼내주고 다녔습니다.

Unable to capture Hong Kil-dong, the king instead arrested Kil-dong's father and threw him in prison.

Upon hearing this news, Kil-dong set to work, making eight scarecrows out of straw. With magic he had learned from the old man with the white beard, he puffed and blew life into them, turning the scarecrows into eight Hong Kil-dongs.

One day, a young man riding a donkey on the road to Seoul loudly announced to one and all that he was Hong Kil-dong.

Anxious to get the reward money, some people jumped him, tied him up securely, and took him to the royal palace.

But then a most unusual thing happened. On the very same day, eight other men calling themselves Hong Kil-dong were caught, bound, and taken to the royal palace.

임금님은 홍길동이 잡히지 않자, 홍길동의 아버지를 잡아 가두게 했습니다.

그것을 안 홍길동은 짚으로 여덟 개의 허수아비를 만들었습니다.

그러고나서 허수아비들에게 '혹' 하고 숨을 불어 넣자, 여덟 개의 허수아비는 여덟 명의 홍길동이 되었습니다.

어느 날, 나귀를 탄 소년이 자기가 홍길동이라고 하면서 서울 거리에 나타났습니다.

사람들은 상을 받으려고 소년을 묶어 대궐로 데려갔습니다.

그런데 이상한 일이 벌어졌습니다.

같은 날 여덟 명의 홍길동이 대궐로 묶여 온 것입니다.

The king summoned Kil-dong's father from his cell and commanded him to identify the real Hong Kil-dong.

"Kil-dong, what's the meaning of all this?" his father asked in confusion. "Hurry up. Step forward and reveal yourself."

Eight men stepped forward, got on their knees to bow, and said, "Father, I take the riches of bad people and give them to the poor. Since I was not entitled to a government job, this is the way I've chosen to carry out justice." After saying these words, all eight rose up into the air and fell on their backs in unison, no longer men but scarecrows.

While the eight scarecrows fell apart, the real Kil-dong ran out into the palace courtyard and suddenly vanished.

임금님은 홍길동의 아버지를 불러 진짜 홍길동을 가려내게 했습니다.

"길동아 이게 무슨 짓이냐? 얼른 모습을 드러내어라."

아버지가 이렇게 꾸짖자, 여덟 명의 홍길동은 똑같이 엎드려 말했습니다.

"아버지, 저는 나쁜 사람들이 모은 재물을 가난한 사람들에게 돌려 주었습니다. 벼슬을 할 수 없었기에 이렇게 제 뜻을 펼쳐야 했습니다."

말을 마친 여덟 명의 홍길동은 '풀썩' 하고 뒤로 자빠졌습니다.

대궐 마당에 있던 홍길동은 온데간데 없고, 여덟 개의 허수아비만 나동그라져 있었습니다.

Knowing that Kil-dong desired a government position, the king thought of a plan. He would grant Kil-dong a position in order to capture him. The new post was proclaimed throughout the land.

A few days later, Kil-dong dressed in splendid clothes and returned to the palace in a palanquin.

Hidden inside the palace, the most trustworthy of the king's soldiers lay in wait to seize Kil-dong. As soon as they made their move, Kil-dong rose up into the air and disappeared in smoke of five colors.

Kil-dong then gathered his band of men and led them across the ocean to a small island. He founded a new nation there which he named Land of Laws. He worked hard for justice and lived happily ever after.

임금님은 홍길동이 벼슬을 하고 싶어 하는 줄 알고 거짓으로 벼슬을 내렸습니다.

며칠 뒤에 옷을 잘 차려 입은 홍길동이 가마를 타고 대궐로 들어왔습니다.

그 때, 대궐 안에 숨어있던 날쌘 군사들이 홍길동을 잡으려고 와락 달려들었습니다.

그러자 홍길동은 몸을 솟구쳐, 오색 연기와 함께 하늘높이 사라졌습니다.

그 뒤에 홍길동은 활빈당 무리를 이끌고 어느 조그만 섬으로 갔습니다.

홍길동은 그 섬에 '율도국' 이라는 나라를 세우고 열심히 일하며 행복하게 살았습니다.

The Man Who Bought the Shade of a Tree

In the hot, humid summer, people like to rest in the cool shade of a tree.

There is a humorous story concerning the shade of a certain tree.

Once upon a time in a small village lived a greedy old rich man.

In front of his house stood a tall elm tree. When summer would come, the old man would spread a mat in the shade of the tree to take a nap.

나무 그늘을 산 총각

무더운 여름이면 사람들은 시원한 나무 그늘을 찾아 땀을 식힙니다.

이 나무 그늘에 얽힌 재미있는 이야기가 있답니다.

옛날 어느 마을에 욕심 많은 부자 영감이 살았습니다.

부자 영감의 집 앞에는 커다란 느티나무가 한 그루 서 있었습니다.

여름만 되면 부자 영감은 느티나무 그늘에 자리를 깔고 낮잠을 자곤 했습니다.

One bright summer's day, a young man who had been working in a field under the hot sun came to the shade of the tree where the rich old man was sleeping and sat down. He rested awhile in the cool shade before the rich old man woke up from his nap.

As soon as he saw the young man, the rich old man began to yell at him in a loud voice. "You rascal, what are you doing here? How can you come to somebody else's shade without permission? Go away and don't come back."

The young man was surprised, but asked politely, "Are you saying this is your shade?"

Growing angrier, the rich old man yelled even louder. "Yes, I'm saying exactly that. The shade of this tree belongs to me."

뙤약볕 아래서 일을 하던 한 총각이 부자 영감이 자고 있는 나무 그늘에 들어와 앉았습니다.

총각이 시원한 그늘에서 한참 쉬고 있는데 부자 영감이 잠에서 깨어 일어났습니다.

부자 영감은 총각을 보자 대뜸 소리를 질렀습니다.

"네 이놈, 왜 남의 그늘에 함부로 들어왔지? 썩 나가지 못해!"

총각은 깜짝 놀라 되물었습니다.

"아니, 영감님의 그늘이라뇨?"

그러나 부자 영감은 더 큰 소리로 말했습니다.

"이 나무 그늘은 내 것이란 말이다!"

"Excuse me, sir," said the young man. "This tree belongs to all the villagers."

"Listen to me," said the rich old man with a sneer. "My grandfather's grandfather planted this tree. I own the shade. Now stop talking nonsense and get out."

The young man felt anger welling up inside him but patiently kept his temper. Soon he came up with a good idea. "Sir," he said, "will you sell the shade of this tree to me?"

At these words, the rich old man's ears perked up. "Certainly, a tree's shade has an owner. And I am the owner of this tree's shade. Give me five copper coins and it's yours."

"영감님, 이 느티나무는 마을 사람들 모두의 나무입니다."

총각이 이렇게 말하자 부자 영감은 코웃음을 치며 말했습니다.

"이놈아, 이 나무는 우리 할아버지의 할아버지께서 심어 놓으신 나무다. 잔말 말고 썩 나가!"

총각은 화가 났지만 꾹 참았습니다. 그리고 한 가지 꾀를 생각해 냈습니다.

"영감님, 이 나무 그늘을 저에게 팔지 않으시겠어요?"

부자 영감은 그 말에 귀가 솔깃해졌습니다.

"아무렴, 나무 그늘도 임자가 있지. 바로 내가 이 나무 그늘의 주인이란 말야. 닷 냥만 내고 사 가게."

The young man promptly took five copper coins from his pocket and handed them to the rich old man.

"There are fools in this world who'll even buy the shade of a tree." the old man said to himself and laughed. Then he rolled up his mat and looked around for the shade of another tree.

The sun was beginning to set, and the shadows were growing longer and longer. The shadow of the elm tree stretched over the wall around the rich old man's house and into his courtyard.

The young man who had been lying down in the shade of the tree got up and followed the shadow into the rich old man's courtyard.

총각은 부리나케 닷 냥을 가져다가 부자 영감에게 주었습니다.

'하하, 나무 그늘을 사는 어리석은 녀석이 다 있구나.'

부자 영감은 자리를 걷어서 다른 나무 그늘을 찾아갔습니다.

해가 기울자, 나무 그늘이 길게 늘어졌습니다.

느티나무 그림자는 부자 영감네 담장을 넘어 안마당까지 드리워졌습니다.

나무 그늘에 누워 있던 총각은 그늘을 따라 부자 영감네 안마당으로 들어갔습니다.

Seeing this, the rich old man screamed at him. "You scoundrel, how dare you enter somebody else's yard? Did I invite you in?"

Without a word, the young man followed the shade of the elm tree and sat down in the rich old man's courtyard. He would not budge an inch. "Sir," he called out. "Didn't you sell me the shade of this tree? And doesn't that mean whatever spot the shade goes to belongs to me?"

The rich old man could not say a word.

총각을 본 부자 영감은 버럭 소리를 질렀습니다.

"이놈아, 왜 남의 집 마당에 함부로 들어오느냐?"

그러자 총각은 부자 영감네 안마당에 드리워진 느티나무 그늘 아래에 떡 버티고 앉아서 말했습니다.

"영감님께서 저에게 이 나무 그늘을 팔지 않으셨습니까? 그러니 그늘이 어디에 생기든지 모두 저의 것이지요."

부자 영감은 아무 말도 하지 못했습니다.

The shadow of the tree grew longer and longer, until it reached inside the rich old man's house. Accordingly, the young man stood up, walked briskly into the house, and lay comfortably down on his back on the polished wooden floor.

The rich old man was so furious that he began to jump up and down in frustration.

Soon the shadow of the tree extended deep into the rich old man's bedroom. The young man opened the bedroom door loudly and stepped noisily into the room.

As soon as the sun set and the shadows disappeared, the young man quickly left the rich old man's house.

The next day and the day after, the young man followed the shadow of the tree into the rich old man's house, going in and out as if it were his own house.

나무 그늘은 점점 길게 늘어져서 부잣집 마루 위에 드리워졌습니다.

총각은 마루 위로 성큼성큼 올라가 벌렁 누웠습니다.

부자 영감은 화가 나서 발을 동동 굴렀습니다.

마침내 그늘은 부잣집 안방까지 깊숙이 들어갔습니다.

총각은 안방 문을 벌컥 열고 저벅저벅 들어갔습니다.

해가 져서 나무 그늘이 사라지자, 총각은 얼른 부잣집을 나왔습니다.

다음 날도 그 다음 날도 총각은 나무 그늘을 따라 부잣집을 자기 집처럼 드나들었습니다.

The rich old man grabbed the young man. "Give me back the shade of the tree," he said, "and I'll give you five copper coins."

"Give back this wonderful shade? Don't be ridiculous."

When the villagers learned that the rich old man was so greedy he would even sell the shade of a tree, they all came around to point him out to their children.

As time went by, the rich old man could no longer bear the situation. One day he left his house, moved far away, and was never heard from again.

The young man acquired the big house without having to pay anything for it.

Thereafter, any villager could go to the shade of the elm tree at any time and rest.

부자 영감은 총각에게 말했습니다.

"닷 냥을 줄 테니 나무 그늘을 돌려 주게."

"이렇게 좋은 그늘을 무르다니요? 어림도 없지요."

총각은 계속 부잣집을 드나들었습니다.

마을 사람들은 부자 영감을 욕심장이 라고 손가락질했습니다.

견디다 못한 부자 영감은 집을 버리고 먼 곳으로 가 버렸습니다.

총각은 큰 집을 거저 얻었습니다.

그 뒤로 마을 사람들은 누구나 느티나무 그늘에서 마음껏 쉴 수 있게 되었습니다.